Praise for Reeni's Turn

"Reeni Rosenbloom leapt off the page and pirouetted straight into my heart. Her struggles with body image and the pressure to conform to society's ideal were both achingly real and refreshingly honest. Every young girl needs to read this lyrical gem of a novel!"

—Jenny Meyerhoff, author of *The Friendship Garden* Series, *The Fantastic Life of Louie Burger* books

"Through beautifully crafted poetry, Carol Coven Grannick creates a main character who is strong yet vulnerable and highly relatable. Reeni's Turn artfully portrays the dance that is middle school—sometimes smooth, sometimes unstable, always growth-rendering."

—Ami Polonsky, author of *Gracefully Grayson* and *Spin With Me*

"Readers will not forget Reeni's passion for dance, her struggles to honor that passion during the turbulence of changes in her life, and her quest to find the balance between body and courage. Carol Coven Grannick is not afraid to show readers a desperate Reeni. But she also gives us the joy of a dancing Reeni. A wonderful story."

—Jacqueline Briggs Martin, *Bim, Bam, Bop...and Oona* and Caldecott award-winning *Snowflake Bentley*

REENI'S TURN

Carol Coven Grannick

Fitzroy Books

Published by Fitzroy Books
An imprint of
Regal House Publishing, LLC
Raleigh, NC 27612
All rights reserved

https://fitzroybooks.com

Printed in the United States of America

ISBN -13 (paperback): 9781646030125
ISBN -13 (hardcover): 9781646030514
ISBN -13 (epub): 9781646030392
Library of Congress Control Number: 2020930424

Interior and cover design by Lafayette & Greene
lafayetteandgreene.com
Cover images © by C.B. Royal

Regal House Publishing, LLC
https://regalhousepublishing.com

Printed in the United States of America

For Bob and Adam

and

in memory of
Miss Frances Allis

"It takes courage to grow up and become who you really are…"

—E.E. Cummings

Daydreaming

My pointe shoes step, step, step,
point-press, point-press, point-press,
silk and wood across the stage,

with only the plink, plank, plunk of harp strings
and rush-rush whisper of a swan's tutu
bouncing against layers of itself,

a tight bodice holding a wild heart inside me
because I am not eleven-year-old Reeni, I am
Odette, Queen of the Swans.

My arms lift like wings,
feathers against my face
like soft wind spinning, turning—

then: *Hey, Reeni! Wake up!*
Rosana shoves my arm
and I bump my chin on the barre,
tug at my tights
as if they need adjustment

and Queen of the Swans
crashes to earth.

Barre

Plié-two-three, up-two-three,
muscle to muscle, a simple knee-bend,
but toes to fingertips move together

as something deep inside somewhere I can't reach
sends a message controlled but loose,
strong but flowing—

Dance!
Music flows through me
like air and blood,

no thoughts, just feelings.
My body moves
like breath.

Lost and Found, Where Lost is Better

We line up five across for a combination.
Dhara outlines her body with smooth hands
that mark a grown-up shape she seems to love.

Lacey'd rather be playing softball, swinging her arms
first-second-third-fourth position
like she wants to hit one out of the park.

Rosana has a permanent pout
because her parents make her dance
(no P.E. at school)

and New Yorker Sasha spends more time
letting us know we're from Chicago
than she does practicing,

black leotard hooked up
on jagged hips the way she says
real dancers do.

Mom found Ms. Allie's for me
when I was four, and this year Ms. Allie said,
Next year you'll need a high-level class I can't provide.

But here's where I learned to dance.
Here's where my body has a voice.
Here's where I want to stay.

Here's where, lost in the music, my body moves
with notes placed perfectly, composing
something beautiful.

Frost

In a minute Ms. Allie's voice peels away my cocoon.
Reeni, come to the front and do it alone,

and a flicker of something
changes inside

like tingling frost
on these winter windows

and the noise begins—
Is my turnout good enough?
Are my arms soft or stiff?
How is my arabesque?

I breathe in, blow out to warm the frost
and try to pretend no one's watching

but everyone is
and my noisy brain and mixed up feet

know it.

Memory—First Recital

I was four, a Raindrop in the line
with Sunshine, Moonglow, Wind, and Air.

Ms. Allie slid me out from backstage,
ballet slippers skating me across smooth wood.

My feet wouldn't walk.

A distant drum-like boom—SPOTLIGHT!
A yellow glow, waiting for me.

I searched for Mom, Dad, Jules
in the audience. I squeaked, *Where are you?*

My baby-sobs exploded, and I flew down steps
at the side of the stage. *Mommy! Daddy!*

Disappearing into their arms
never wanting to dance again,

the music began
and I wished, wished, wished
I could be back on stage.

Up and Down

Sasha watches me
from behind. Up
and down.

Her mirror-eyes show me
she's looking
up
and
down
the back of me,

eyes running
speeding up
and down.

Staring

My feet inch forward
off-rhythm.

Ms. Allie says, *Reeni*
pay attention please!

I want to say,
Tell her to stop looking at me!

but instead I stare
at the cracks in the floor

then remind myself
I may not look like Sasha

but I dance the way
she wishes she could.

Backbend Without Hands

No music, we settle into quiet stretches
before standing for backbends without hands,
one at a time.

Ms. Allie faces me, circling my back,
not holding, but tapping with her finger
at
the
lowest
point
of
my
spine.
She says, *Right here, I'm right here.*

I backward-bend slowly
smoothly
half a circle
tracing my head
to the floor

all moving muscle, no thoughts, no words,
Ms. Allie urging, gentle,

there if I need her,
steady, strong,
safe in the circle
of her untouching arms.

Reflection

Changed and ready, waiting for Dad with the car
crawling through March snow to pick me up.

Snow turns to slush as the window shines my reflection.
The barre lets me lean in, press, lift, stretch my leg
into arabesque,

my pointed toe with shoe
rising behind my head

when Ms. Allie walks in. *Reeni, you're here.*
Oh, good. My leg returns to earth. She takes my hand.

I want you to solo this year for my last recital.
Choreograph your own dance, music of your choice.

My body burns then ices over.
Me? A solo?
I want to! But I can't!

Wait—*your* last *recital?*
She pulls my chin up to look at her.
Reeni, I'm retiring after this year.

I stare and stare. I'm frozen in place.
Where will I go?
What will I do?

I shake my head. I can't. I can't.
I'll slide to the floor if she drops my hands

but a still, small voice inside me says
Yes
and I say it out loud.

Memory—The Still, Small Voice

Last fall on Yom Kippur,
my first time in adult services,
I held the heavy prayer book instead of stapled pages,

let my mind wander
the way it does when I'm dancing,
swaying from a long time standing,

swaying to familiar melodies of prayers.
Then these words:
The great shofar is sounded,
a still, small voice is heard.

My body stilled,
the words shivered into my heart
and through my body—brain, heart, arms and legs,

the way music does,
deep inside where it sings out,
Dance!

But instead of that,
these words whispered to me,

Listen!

The Loud, Huge Voice

When I think about being the center of attention
my Loud, Huge Voice drowns out Still and Small.

It shouts from somewhere outside: "Watch out!
Be afraid!"
It writes imaginary news reports that mock me.

"Last night the dance world saw the debut of Reeni
Rosenbloom. Sources tell us she practices endlessly,
but this reporter doesn't see any proof whatsoever.
The young allegedly gifted dancer entered from stage
left, tripped, and fell on her face. We have to ask,
why did her teacher put her in this embarrassing
position?"

It's About Time

I text Beck my good news
and nightmare all at once

and she texts back
what best friends do.

Yay! UR fantastic! Don't worry!

But her words don't steady me
the way they usually do.

Instead I tip and teeter,
off-

balance.

Old

Dad and I stomp in through our heavy front door.
Warm and cozy, old carved lamp, shabby-soft couch,

Great-Grandma's furniture. My little-girl reading place,
snuggled up with Mom under old quilts
or Great-Grandpa's army blanket.

Dinner cooking in Great-Grandma's heavy pots,
her pink and grey table set for dinner.

They're part of my history, Mom says.
No need to waste them, Dad says.

This is my home,
supporting me like a barre
comforting me like music.

Like Me, Like Her

Plates on the table, blue glass,
odd silverware collected for fun.

Mom's at her tiny kitchen desk
in the corner, grading a thick stack of papers,

twirling a curl that matches mine,
rubbing her eyes, yawning.

Music from *Swan Lake* swirls in my head.
I'll choreograph three minutes from a pas de deux.

Mom moves with her own rhythm,
her fingers' choreography,

a smile, a frown,
she scribbles comments
with a green pen,

rereads and nods,
smoothing the paper to finish,
nods again, like a curtsy

to finish.

Leaning Toward Jules

Outside Jules' room I sway
toward the open space,

a door slightly open,
a sister lately too busy for me.

I touch the door and push it open
the way I've always done

but she snaps, *Reeni!*
I'm busy! Leave me alone!

Pleased to Inform You

Last Thanksgiving weekend, The Letter arrived:
"We are pleased to inform you…"

Jules jumped and screamed and ran to the kitchen.
I got in! I'm going! With a scholarship, too!

I didn't have to ask. My sick stomach told me
it was University of Michigan.

Not too far away for her.
But too far away for me
not to feel sister-less.

Memory—Thanksgiving

Thanksgiving was my favorite holiday
until that day last November.

Jules used to say, *I'm grateful for Reeni*
until last Thanksgiving when all she said was,

I'm grateful I got into Michigan!
I can't wait to get to college!

and a rock in my throat made me choke
on Thanksgiving turkey.

Something New at Dinner

Now Jules blabs at dinner like a battery-charged doll
I got the part! Another starring role! Senior play!
A Midsummer Night's Dream!

Blah. Blah. Blah.
Her part's a tall, thin girl named Helena.
And when Jules' battery finally runs down

my snarky voice says, *What a surprise.*
I shock myself. Everyone stares.
Their eyes say, *Reeni, you don't talk like that!*

I blurt out, *Ms. Allie asked me to solo and I said yes.*
Eyebrows up, Dad says my baby name, *Reeni-Beeni,*
reaches out to squeeze my hand.

Mom hugs me close all warm and tight.
So happy for you, sweet girl.

I make a face at Jules.
My hands are shaking as I think,
I can be in the spotlight, too!

Jules in the Light

Jules glows.
Dad calls her a born performer
loving the spotlight
shining as if the light's inside.

Jules gets bouquets
at the end of every show—
she's Dorothy, Peter Pan, Annie.

I was always little sister, glowing in her light,
trailing after, proud to be with her.

Jules is your sister? You lucky girl!

Glowing in her light,
second place was enough.

Glowing in her light—
I never cared

until this year
when she grew up too much

and left me
in shadows.

Dancing Place, Dancing Space

Dad made the studio down in our basement,
open space for leaping, twirling, wood floor for bounce,
mirrors and barre, big cushion in the corner.

Cartoonist and carpenter, he says
an artist must have a place to practice, create
for a world in need of beautiful things.

He says we're the same, both needing to do that.
You danced in your crib, all fingers and toes.
I think Shakespeare had people like you in mind when he said
"There was a star danced, and under that was I born."

I want to believe a day will come
when I'll lose my fear of dancing for others,
like I lose myself and find myself

whenever I dance alone.

Choreography

Three minutes from *Swan Lake,*
a pas de deux, played again and again.
Listen, listen, lean and dream...

I'm onstage alone as the spotlight glows,
fear of the audience scatters like stage dust.
Breathing deeply, air circles around me

bending with me, cushioning each move
and my heart stretches to fill me,
hold me

close to the world
right up against
the edges of the sky.

Goodnight

Mom and Dad come upstairs
to kiss me goodnight. Am I too old for that?

Dad kisses my cheek. *Night, Reeni-Beeni.*
Mom whispers, *Sleep tight, Reeni-Beeni.*

Mom's in the doorway
the light on her hair.

*Mom, could you and Dad stop
calling me Reeni-Beeni now?*

Her smile turns sad
when she says, *Yes, we'll try.*

I hurt her feelings.
I should take it back.

But I don't.

Tight

This morning my T-shirt seems like it's for someone else.
I tug it off, stare at my chest and its little hills.

I pull my door open—*Mom!*—but Jules comes in.
I shove her away and slam the door—*Stay out!* I yell,

grab Dad's old U. of I. shirt I sleep in,
shake it open to pull it on

and it billows when I pull it over my head,
then flutters and settles, a big sad sigh against my chest.

Mom Says

Remember we talked about how girls change?
That's what this is. You're filling out, getting hips and breasts.

She says we'll buy a bra
and I say, *Ugh. Do we have to?*

Then I check myself in the mirror
and growl, *Okay.*

You're growing into your woman's body, Mom says.
I scowl. *I'm growing out of my clothes!*

Beck and I

Lunch is our time together during the day.
We fast-walk, lunch bags slapping,

to old tables, scratched, patched,
benches worn smooth from sitting

and sliding. We're at the same table,

hungry to talk
as if we've been starving.

I tell her about the morning.
I'm getting fat!

She shrugs. *Mom says we all gain weight
in puberty,*

mocking the way her pediatrician mom
says *puberty.* My parents say so too

and I never had a different thought
till now, like a flipped switch in my brain.

I thought I'd grow up taller and thinner.
What if I don't look like a ballerina?

Beck smiles like everyone knows the answer:
You dance like one.

This Year

All year I've been hearing that

everyone hates
their thighs
butts
legs
arms.

And everything they hate
they call 'fat'.

Fat is not a size to them.
Fat = bad.

The only thing that isn't
'fat' is their hair
but they hate that,
too.

Their words make me squirm
like some secret
I haven't told myself.

Sixth Grade

I duck into math, eyes down
counting squares on the floor

not wanting looks.

Sixth grade's weird
when you're the youngest,

sizes and colors
of clothes and hair and even some faces

with lipstick, eye shadow
sneaked on in the bathroom away from home,

noisier, smellier—perfume, sweat—
cell phones dropped in a box when school starts.

I'm in way over my head.
Huge waves of sixth graders

knock me around
when I'm just trying

to wade in.

Homework

Back at home I zip through work sheets,
click to YouTube and search for Sixth Grade

and the first thing I see is "survival kit"
with a hand that has yellow nail polish with red dots

taking out a bottle of perfume, deodorant,
a pad or tampon for your period if you get it,
cotton balls, bandages, alcohol wipes, lotion,
lip gloss, makeup, hand sanitizer.

Mom talked to me about everything
I need to know about all this stuff

and the no-lipstick-no-crazy-nail polish rule,
but they don't have to worry.

My survival kit is clean leotards
and soft, worn leather pink ballet shoes.

Downstairs

I move through the music.
The center's here, here near my heart
and lower down, strong muscles that hold me.

Something mysterious, deep inside
captures the music, sends it through,
makes me fly.

Music erases sixth grade worries,
erases everything but itself
as my body fills the empty space

with dance.

On the Way to Hebrew School

Grandma would want you to,
Mom and Dad remind me about Hebrew school,

about learning Hebrew and Jewish traditions
and having a bat mitzvah sooner than I want to.

What if I decide I don't want a bat mitzvah?
They look shocked that I've asked.

We'd like you to have one—it's the Jewish way
you change from girl to woman.

My face burns.
Words disappear.
I didn't say

I'm changing already.

Together

Beck and Jason,
sit together in Hebrew school.

I slide into my desk
next to them

waiting for Mr. Hirschman,
looking at Jason

each time he looks
away.

I Hate YouTube

I search YouTube
when Mom's not watching,

cold and shaking
in my warm house

and find Rapid Weight Gain
and Preteen Girls.

Mom is right.
Bodies get bigger.

I swallow a scream, punch out of YouTube
and pound up the stairs

as Mom calls, *What's wrong, Reeni?*
and I don't answer.

I can't explain
how I suddenly don't recognize
my body

and how not recognizing
is turning to
not liking.

My World Should Be Flat

Dancers pose
in posters on my walls,

chests flat,
tummies flat,
hair straight and flat.

Dance floor flat.
Flat, flat, flat.

Jules is flat.
Flat, flat, flat.

Flat as Jules, flat as Jules,
I've got to stay as flat as Jules.

Am I?

Mom, am I fat?
I'm at the hall mirror, see her behind me.

She catches my eyes.
If you mean "fat" as in "bad," the answer will always be "No."
Your body is changing and it's perfectly normal.

Did she hear what I asked?
Just tell me the truth!

You're strong and you're healthy.
You're an average size—rounder than some, less round than others.
Bigger than some, less big than others.
Your size is not a prize or a punishment.

She's behind me faster than I can turn,
hands on my expanding hips.
No dieting, Reeni.
You're beautiful just as you are.

I nod and head back to my room.
Strong and healthy is all that counts?

I don't think Mom heard the news
from sixth grade.

Pimple

Great. Now I've got a pimple?
When I'm just eleven?

I smush my face into the mirror,
examine
poke
squeeze—

Oh no! now it's
BIGGER!

Mom!
Mo-o-o-m!
MOM!

Mom's Hands

Mom's here in a minute,
opens the door, whispers,
Take your hands away, sweetheart,
and let me see.

Then with a pat on my hand she's gone—
Be right back.
Now she's here with a new soap and soft white washcloth.
We'll keep it clean. That's the best thing to do.

Her hands smooth warm water and soap
on the ugly thing, ugly me,
then over my face,
she's gentle as the soft center of my solo.

I babble and whine,
Why is this happening to me?
Is this another wonderful part of becoming a woman?

She strokes my face with warm water,
doesn't answer my question but makes me feel
that I must be less ugly than I think.

Bigger Everyday

How can my chest
get bigger every day?
My hips, my thighs, my butt
all bigger and rounder?

Am I imagining this?
Everything's showing,
everything's curving
even in the biggest shirt I find

it's all over the place—
there, there,
here
and there!

I'd Like To Be Invisible

At school my desk
feels smaller,
my thighs spread out
in the plastic chair

a hand over my pimple
that Mom said not to touch
so now I'm making it worse.

I'm disgusting.
I'm sure I'm disgusting.
I tighten my muscles,
squeeze my strong
'fat'
legs
together
and try to tell myself
that 'fat' is not 'bad'.

Smaller Than I Am

Beck and I—
we're eye to eye

but when we high-five
her little hand whacks half of mine.

Her shoes
slip neatly into mine.

We never thought
it was anything but fun.

All of a sudden
I ask, *How come you're not having 'rapid weight gain'?*

P.E.

Inside today,
late winter hail banging at the windows

wall hooks piled with tossed clothes.
Chatter hits and stings like the hail.
I hate my stomach.
My thighs are disgusting.
I'm SO going on a diet.
I'm fat—you're NOT fat—but I am.
You're NOT—look at THIS.

Words pound, pound, pound
and force me to listen,

unfamiliar, odd
but heavy and hurting
as if I'm standing outside
in the storm

where no one has heard
that 'fat' isn't 'bad'.

Noise

Lunchroom noise swarms. Beck's talking
but I'm trying to hear Dani, Makela, and Amaya.

Dani's got a brochure from the nurse's office
with pictures and lists of "good" and "bad" foods.

Makela wants to lose a whole size by summer
and has decided not to eat cheese.

Amaya hates her thighs and her round face
and is swearing off sweets.

Hey! Beck pulls my hand. *Stop listening to that!*
I stare at her and force a smile

but I can't stop listening and my body leans
toward the ones who sound like I've begun to feel.

Inside Ballerina

I always thought I'd grow like Jules,
my body like hers, tall and thin.
But instead I look like Mom and her mom,
sturdy and strong, short and curly.

In class I see Ms. Allie's size
differently, as if it's new,
round body wrapped in a rainbow skirt
tucked up for dancing.

She demonstrates steps as softly as water flows
and when I watch her my heart
begins to dance, too.

When I was four I hid in her skirts
as she made a place for me at the barre
and touched my chin to lift it up.

You're a dancer, dear.
I can see it inside.

But now inside
isn't all that matters.

Now I wonder
if her size is the reason
Ms. Allie doesn't perform.

Practice, Practice, Practice

One hundred pliés.
One hundred rond de jambe.
One hundred battement
till my leg cramps and burns but I'm

practicing
practicing
practicing

as the Still, Small Voice
whispers, *Keep working, Reeni*

but the Loud, Huge Voice
interrupts with, "UGLY!"

Wish I Could

Upstairs, I'm outside her room.
Jules is at rehearsal.

Next year, it will be
all-the-time empty

and that feels as if I'm leaping
and the floor opens up under me,

flying
with no place to land.

Shabbat

At least tomorrow we'll have Shabbat dinner,
our time together.

Our grandparents did
and theirs did, too.

Dad says these rituals
are part of our lives

even though
we're not *completely observant.*

Each Friday night
as Shabbat comes

the day quiets down
for a little while

and we're always here,
close together.

Friday Night

It's a once-a-week rush
when I open the back door

and invisible whiffs of long-roasted chicken
swirl around and pull me into an almost-Shabbat place,

Mom's soup-of-the-week
simmers and steams.

Hurry! Wait—
tuck schoolbooks away,

find a clean shirt, maybe a skirt,
wash my face, hear Jules rush in

and head downstairs—ready,
ready, wait.

Ssssttt! Mom strikes the match,
touches wicks, curved hands circle in front of the flames

pulling in light, blessing burning candles.
Shabbat is here.

Blessing

Jules and I bow our heads, parents' fingers
curve over them.

They're blessing us
with ancient Hebrew words, then English, too:

May you be like Sarah, Rebecca, Rachel, and Leah.
May God bless you and guard you.
May God show you favor and be gracious to you.
May God show you kindness and grant you peace.

I don't know about God, but I feel certain about
my parents' hands, soft as the blessing,
and candlelight, homemade challah, wine and juice,
and the four of us together.

And now the sound
of the Still, Small Voice
hugs and holds me, whispers,

Listen!
as I wonder
what the new week will bring.

Stars

I beg to go to the mall with Beck.
Dad drops us off for an hour, no more.

I scan tiaras for my solo on May 27th.
Beck arranges one
in my masses of frizz and blah-brown curls.

She makes a face.
I don't think you're a tiara girl.
She finds some stars,
blue and silver, shining against a purple card.

These, she says,
and I agree.

Beck always knows
what's best for me.

Not the Same

We stop for hot chocolate and Beck sketches a flower
on her napkin. The lines appear like magic,
soft and curvy, petals resting inside each other
like tired best friends—a rose.

I tell Beck I'm scared I'll change my mind
about the solo. She huffs and says,
Enough already!

I'm mad. *Remember when Ms. Johnson*
hung your painting
and you were so embarrassed?

It's not the same at all, Beck says.
I had no choice.
And besides,
I never told her to take it down.

Magazines

I break Dad's rule to stop nowhere before dance class,
sneak into the bodega, an evil character in a ballet,

slide to the magazine racks,
where covers show bodies with big breasts,

bodies with no breasts, thin bodies, thinner,
pictures of cupcakes, then diet advice.

Get thin without dieting!
Lose weight and gain confidence!

I'm searching, searching
for a body that looks like mine

but my breath comes too fast to know what I'm doing
and my wet, shaking hands ruin corners of pages

so I now have to buy them,
hide them in my backpack.

Popping Out

The pimple is bigger, bright red.
Pimple! Get lost!
A new shirt's too tight.
My mirror's a carnival funhouse reflection
that shrinks, grows, and shows me myself
in weird, morphing ways.

Bra

If there's something worse than being watched
while I dance

it would be this moment,
this one right now
in this dressing room
with Mom and some strange woman
who measures me right underneath
then smiles and shouts out "32 A"
with comments about my "cute little figure!"

as if we were onstage
with an audience of strangers who shout,
Here she is! Look at her!
A brand-new woman!
The crowd laughs
and Reeni Rosenbloom slides
into
a hole
in the ground

and barely fits.

Reflection

In the morning I don't recognize
the roundish girl in the clear glass window

but I see the bra through her shirt
and I feel her body burning, churning

as Jason struts closer to that girl who's me,
calling *Reeni, hey Reeni, wearing something new today?*

I can't find words, but my body folds in
like Maya Plisetskaya's "Dying Swan" on YouTube,

except
unbeautifully.

My Inside Voice

Wish I could yell it, scream it, shout it:
why are you saying that, creepy boy?

I hate you. Hate, hate you.
Never going to talk to you.

Never going to look at your
stupid silky red hair and turn-my-heart freckles.

But my inside voice
stays where it lives.

The Loud, Huge Voice

"Last night the dance world saw the debut of Reeni Rosenbloom but unfortunately the dance world saw more than her debut. As the spotlight glowed the dancer lifted her eyes to us, raised an arm and split her costume! The top unraveled and revealed her size 32A bra and two RAPIDLY GROWING BREASTS!!!! When interviewed afterwards Ms. Rosenbloom seemed unable to speak. We recommend that she choose a new career path. Very, very quickly."

Crisscross

Arms snap into crisscross
against my books,
across my chest
smashing me
ouching me
into a desk,
a hard plastic desk,
leaning low
bowing down
my chin cupped against
crisscrossed arms.

In the Halls

Dani and I walk from science to math
and an older boy pulls at Dani's glittery shirt

and the bra strap that shows.
Ooh, sparkly! Can I have some of that?

She slaps his stupid hand away.
She says, *He does that all the time.*

I stop at my locker to pull on my sweatshirt
so the bra hides inside

like a heavy curtain
in front of the stage of me.

Clipped

Worry-free downstairs
dancing alone,
freedom like a bird taking off
for a joyride, no landing place in mind,

inside from heart to muscles
and through each part of me—
fly!

Muscles move me up, down, around
and I dance, dance, dance,
grow wings and then

the Loud, Huge Voice shouts
"Fat!"
(*Bad!*)

and I hide
in the corner
away from my dancing self,

wings clipped.

Outside

After class Ms. Allie watches my solo,
suggests an extra turn, a stronger point,
then hugs me close.

I'm shaking, anticipating an audience.
I try to draw courage from her hug
but can't stop trembling.

Sweat dripping, off to change,
I hear Sasha.
Reeni's a little chubby to be a swan.

You're just jealous. It's Dhara now.
You're so skinny a pencil would seem fat to you.
My eyes cloud up.
My ears roar.

Get me out.
Get me out.
Get me out.

As Fast As Possible

I stare at the floor as if it will help me disappear
but when it doesn't, step into the changing room,
grab my jacket
pull my backpack
out of the corner
rip my jeans and T-shirt
off the hook

push past Sasha and Dhara
and

run, run, run.

Try Not

Each foot near
but not in a puddle

each square of sidewalk
full of tiny pebbles

swimming through my wet eyes
can't count them, can't count them.

Don't want to think about
Sasha's whispered words.

Don't want to think
about lunch talk at school.

Don't want to think
at all.

The Word

It circles around me
like cold wet wind
in Chicago's almost-Spring.

Chubby. Chubby. Chubby.

The word tugs and knots
like a winter scarf
and scratches my ears:

Chubby. Chubby. Chubby.

It breaks up and sounds like
a fake word

CHUH. Bee.
Ch. Uh. Bee.
*Chu*bby.

Just a word.
But now it's ugly.
Just like "fat".

And it's about me.

Not Today

Mom's grading papers and she's up from her desk
when she sees my face, but *No Not Now!* I yell
and race upstairs, slam my door, dump my backpack
a huge pressing lump inside my throat
keep myself from ripping posters off the wall,
skinny ballerinas whose bodies I imagined

would be mine one day.

Naked

I strip off tights and leotard,
stare at bumps and bulges.

Too wide. Too big.
Too round. Too much.

Mom says *womanly*.
I say *ugly*.

Mom says *different sizes*.
Almost everyone else says *bad!*

Expectations

Jules pushes my door open
What's wrong with you?

Can't help it:
I blurt out Sasha's words.

She wrinkles her nose
and says, *Not nice,*
and my anger floats toward loving her

but she turns to her books and phone
pulls a strand of hair into place
says *Well you know
you don't have to dance the solo.*

No one expects you to be a star,
she says. *No one says you have to do it.*

Worst Big Sister

I'm speechless, as usual
except to myself:
No one expects you to be a star.
No one says you have to do it.

Why did she say that?
Does she think I can't do it?
I hate her for real.
She thinks she's so great
and I'm so...nothing?
She's meaner than mean. She's horrible. Selfish.
I can't wait until she's gone!
Need-to-cry sobs cramp up my throat.

I kick my door, grab a pencil
and start to scratch a deep cut in the wood
but instead press all my anger into the pencil
so I don't ruin the floor

and it breaks into pieces
in my sweaty cramped hands.

Dinner

Dinner is Dad's steamy-spicy
creamy tomato soup,
perfect for a grey, rainy day,
cheese all melty
on crunchy brown bread.

I can't eat this stuff, I say.
I pass the plate to Jules.
I have to lose weight.
Dad puts half a sandwich on my plate.
That's ridiculous.

Mom's louder than usual.
I told you, Reeni, we don't do diets.
You have a healthy relationship with food.
You dance every day.
Your body will settle right where it belongs.

I hear her. The words sound right.
But do they hear me?
I can't wait for my body
to *settle right where it belongs.*

Promises

YouTube again.
This girl says:
You'll feel better.
You'll be calmer.
You'll stop worrying about people looking.

That's what I need!

I zip my jeans.
Tug my shirt.
Grab a mirror,
angle it to see my butt.

Do I really look like that?

Dad's making dinner, Mom's grading papers.
I head down to the computer, search: lose weight fast.

Fingers rushing fingers ready to click
someone's name with a lot of initials
and again I see, "Losing weight will make you more
confident."
I'm hungry for that.

So it says,
eat lots of veggies to feel full
drink tons of water
get tempting foods out of the way
stay busy

eat from a plate
write down what you eat
make a note how you're feeling

But I already
eat lots of vegetables
and drink tons of water.
I don't know what foods to keep "out of the way"
and I'm already busy,
already eat from plates
and before I eat
I feel hungry!

And Also

How can you want something so badly
and also be so afraid to do it?

How can you be so sure you are good at something
and also feel clumsy and inept?

How can you feel so free when you dance alone
and also so tied in knots when people watch?

How can you want this more than anything
but know that to do it you might have to become

somebody you're not?

Write About a Significant Memory

An English essay question:
write about a good or bad memory.

I wonder if what Jules said
is a memory yet or is it still happening

as it returns to play
over and over in my aching brain

and tells me I'd better
write about something else.

Memory—There Was A Time

I was little, and Dad watched while I ran
outside to meet Jules, walking home from school.

She'd turn away from friends
to catch me in a hug, and didn't care

if they laughed at her.
She'd take my hand, swing it,

and we'd skip up the walk,
back home together.

Day One

Stomach growling, I sort through lunch
and toss what I think isn't diet food.

Bread goes first. I sniff it before
I mush it into a ball and roll it aside

and now know what the YouTube diet lady meant
when she talked about "tempting" foods

because now a plain piece of bread
I've eaten every day of my life

feels like it is some amazing
gourmet item from an upscale store

where we don't shop.

Advice

In gym Dani switches gym-shirt-to-school-shirt
faster than her *heads up!* in volleyball.

She pulls on sparkles. She sees my stare.
I know, I know. But I like the sparkle shirts.

I stuff
Dani's words
into my backpack

trying to crumple them
like gym clothes.

Day Two

All kinds of advice at the lunch table today:
Yes to my apple, no to my almonds.

What are you doing?
Beck grabs the container I've shoved away.

I ignore her, scrape tuna off the bread
with insides so empty they ache

and a turning, twisting stomach
that's begging for food.

Day Three

Dani says, *you'll get used to it.*

I munch as slowly as I can:
two rolled-up turkey slices
a pickle
a small apple
huge gulps of water.

Dani's so happy that her jeans are loose.
Amaya fits into an old smaller skirt.
Makela says she ran faster today on the inside track.
My heart pumps a rhythm,
me too I hope,
me too I hope,
me too I hope.

Beck scowls
and reads her book.

But I can practically feel myself
shrinking.

Day Four

I made a sun butter sandwich
because Mom left it out

and I'm as empty as a pit by lunchtime
but get the feeling

the others will tell me it's not diet food,
so I hide in a hallway and gobble it down.

Beck finds me.
What is the matter with you?

Leave me alone, I snap at her,
mouth full.
And she does.

Success, I Think

I'm hungry. So hungry.
But I can wiggle a finger in my waistband
even though the top of me keeps growing.

I'm thinner I'm sure.
I'm thinner I think.
I'm thinner I hope.

But hungry. So hungry.

Practice, Practice, Practice Again

Over
and over and over
after class, after homework

I do barre,
I stretch,
I practice my solo

until my leg cramps and burns—
shake it out,
shake it out!

Practice doesn't seem
to push away
my fear

even though I think
I'm a little thinner.

Busy, Dizzy

Reeni, please come up and set the table.
I mumble, *In a minute. I'm busy.*

What's for dinner?
How will I not eat it?
Am I really losing weight?
How long will this take
to "be more confident"?

I blow out a breath.
Busy, busy. Brain so busy.
Reeni, come upstairs—now!

I'm starving. So hungry.
I can't do this diet.
I'm eating the bread I stashed from my lunch.

Stomp up the stairs
lost in a maze
not sure which direction's
the way I should go
which way I should
turn:

so
dizzy.

Where's Jules?

Where's Jules?
At rehearsal.
She might be late.
There's always a reason—
rehearsal,
study groups
boyfriend,
like she's not part of us
anymore.

I slam plates down on the kitchen table.
Please don't slam the plates, Dad says.

But I do, and bang one down, twirling it, too
and it spins off the table
onto the floor, smashing

into broken bits.

No, It's Not!

Dad hands me the broom, holds the dustpan,
touches my shoulder.
It's hard to think about having her gone next year.

He reaches to hug me. I shake him off, yell,
*No! it's! not! It's annoying. She thinks she's so great
and she doesn't have to do
anything
around
here
any
more!*

Shards of the smashed plate flare out
in a pattern
we scoop up.
Shattered insides
still a mess.

Shabbat on a Diet

Dad's roast chicken with caramelly carrots,
slithery onions, creamy-crunchy potatoes,

homemade challah baked each week
after the deadline for his cartoons.

Candle lighting time. Mom's hands circle the light,
candles flicker, Jules rushes in clattering, chattering,

ducks her head for the blessing,
sisters together just barely.

I mumble *Shabbat Shalom*, don't kiss anyone
and while we eat, I hope no one notices

potatoes and challah
untouched on my plate.

First Job

The good part of busy-busy Jules
is that I get her babysitting job down the block
with four-year-old Serena I've known all her life.
Will I be good? Will I know what to say?

Heart speedy, hands sweaty, grabbing books
off my shelves I'll bring to read.
Dad walks with me. I ring the bell.
My Still, Small Voice says, *Breathe, breathe.*

Dad kisses my cheek. *I'll be back at nine.*
Serena's on the couch. *Reeni! That's in my name, too!*
Read me a story! I love love love stories!
Her mom smiles and takes me aside.

She gives me instructions.
You can count on me to keep her safe, I say.
Serena's mom looks surprised in a good way,
and I am, too!

Serena makes babysitting easy.
We're reading ballet books.
She asks me to show her
all five dance positions

and it's funny how this little girl
makes me feel
so grown up,
so much a ballerina.

Lunch Fight

Makela, Amaya, Dani and I compare our diets.
Beck flips through a book then slams it down.

This is so stupid!
She fixes on my eyes as if she's saying, *You'd better stop.*

Beck bags her lunch and bolts from the table.
I start after her

then change my mind, slide over
closer to Dani, Makela, Amaya

and force a smile when I say
I hate my stomach, too

and they smile back.

At the Whiteboard

Math problems on the board
are as foggy as my brain

but if I blink I'll spill
the stinging tears

and everyone will see
so I stare and stare

at one spot on the board
as if I am beginning a series of turns

but my hand won't write
and when Mr. Salazar says, *Reeni sit down,*

my eyes pour.
I can't turn around,

go back to my desk
but I can't stand up here either,

frozen, squeezing my eyes
as if I can disappear the tears

without anyone seeing.
Head down, frizz in my face

rubbing my eyes as if they itch
I sidestep back and slide

into my desk, slam
my knees against the top

so I can cry
for a reason.

Alone

After school I text Beck.
No answer.

At Hebrew school she walks away
when I ask why she's mad.

I'm spinning without
a place to spot,

a point to keep me steady.

Jason on the Way Out

I refuse to look when Jason slides next to me,
says, *I like the pointe shoe on your jeans.*

I sewed the pointe shoe patch on
just for me at the bottom of my jeans.

I wish I could say, *How come you're nice to me here,
but make stupid comments in school?*

It's cool, he says, shakes that thick silky hair
and I push out a smile. Is he making fun of me?

I hope he can't see the whirling confusion inside me
the way he saw the hidden pointe shoe.

Nothing Worse

I want to tell Beck
about Jason

but can't.

Not talking to her
makes a sound

like the Hebrew homework
I rip in half.

Close

After dinner Mom and Dad
start after me to watch me rehearse.

I mumble, *Not yet*
and escape to the basement.

When I was four and five and six
I'd show them my dances,

only them and Jules and sometimes Beck.
Mom would sing while I spun around,

Little dancing Reeni girl
Sway and swirl, whirl and twirl
Little dancing Reeni girl.

I'd spin across the room
and back
but never far from their hugging arms.

Sad Dance

My body's dragging, pulling.
Steps pour out
like slow tears, missing Beck

and instead of dipping a curtsy at my solo's end
I huddle in the corner
on the big, soft cushion

in the space
that was sometimes
hers.

Can't Sleep

How can someone understand you
all the time

then not?

How can you recognize yourself
all the time

then not?

How can you feel like everything's fine
most of the time

and then because you're growing,
looking different

and people use a word
one stupid word,

everything's
totally
completely
horribly

not?

No Answers

When I dance the solo, what if I fall?
And everyone laughs?

And I run off the stage?
And I hide in the curtains?

And no one can find me?
And I can't go home, ever?

And I don't even have
a best friend's house to go to?

Icky-Sticky Yummy

Serena's mom left all the stuff
for baking rice and marshmallow treats—

Serena calls them *icky-sticky yummy.*
I gather supplies. She waits without squirming.

The stainless bowl
is cold against our hands

as we dig into the gooey mix.
Fingers entwined, Serena's mouth open,

ready for a taste
but I shake my head,

laughing and pressing her little hands
as I scrape off rice and marshmallows

then try to get it off my own.

Now! I say. Time to lick our fingers,
wash and dry hands, then press into the pan,

shove it in the fridge
for minutes that Serena spends

jumping up and down now
wiggling hands and arms and legs

before we edge it out
without cutting into hunks

of *icky-sticky yummy*
sweet.

I'm Sure

I'm sure *icky-sticky-yummy*
isn't on my diet.

Why did I have to eat them
last night

as if they jumped into my mouth
and I had no control?

I should probably not eat for two days
but the thought makes me slide

into the aisles
of the corner bodega

stick my fingers into the deep pocket
where I shoved babysitting money

slink down the aisles
grabbing cookies, caramels, pretzels,

suddenly treasures instead of food
I'll stash in my room, under my bed.

I pay and put three pennies change
in the plastic box for hungry children.

Ten dollars gone?
Diet cheating costs so much!

Perfect Fit

Mom and Dad won't talk
about the money it takes

to buy ballet slippers
to keep me dancing while I grow,

new tights and leotard too.
But I see the prices and feel bad.

Wanting what we can't afford,
I dance through racks of colors—
red and blue, pink, orange, purple—

silks and glitter
tutus and dance skirts

jazz clothes, pointe shoes.
Pointe shoes: when will I get them?

I'm dizzy with pictures in my brain
of whirling, twirling fouettés

and the store starts tipping,
the lights haze over…

Reeni, sit down.

The saleswoman pulls tissue
from soft pink ballet shoes
making a *shshrunch* sound
and in goes my foot,
covered with tights—cool, snug,

hugging my feet, the soft pink leather
begs to be worked.

I press my foot into a point
and she smiles.
Perfect fit, perfect point.

A Lie Like a Sandwich

Reeni, you're skimping on lunch!
Mom reaches around me, lifts slices of turkey.

I stare at my sandwich and turn away
but she holds two slices in front of my face

and I grab them, toss them in foil,
hands fumbling, I'm grumbling,

grabbing, pulling—
Yes! Okay! I promise I'll eat it!

But my lie, like my sandwich, won't satisfy
and I leave for school with Mom's eyes

begging for truth.

Where Am I?

Beck's sketching
on a stack of napkins
one after the other
lines become forms.

Her hands shape snapshots
from her brain:
flowers, horses,
snow-capped mountains.

She used to draw me
dancing
but now she sketches
everything else but.

All Wrong

I hang back when we line up for bourrée turns.

Then I'm in sous-sus position,
half-pointe, tight fifth position, elbows in.

I feel the rush and choose what I'll spot,
Ms. Allie's smile, the prize for a perfect turn.

The tenth snap around my eyes switch
away to the mirror for less than a second

and I stumble,
hop,
try to spin,
                                        the floor's like water
I'm off-
                        balance
and
stumble
again—
Ms. Allie catches me before I fall
                        and moves me to the barre.

Hot and sure I'm turning red
my Loud, Huge Voice shouts deep inside:

"You can't turn right
when you don't spot right!"

Like a Rock

Ms. Allie says something I don't hear.
Dizzy, shaking, so hungry, no lunch.

My head on the barre
body full of empty

but heavy, so heavy.
Stuck on the ground.

She calls Mom to pick me up.
She whispers something on the phone.

Hungry

White-yellow cheese sticks and oranges,
smooth green pears, crisp apples, bananas
wait in a bowl on the table at home.
A plate of dark brown seedy crackers,
a small dish of almonds to crunch.

My stomach's an empty balloon.
I need food like air.
But I don't dare take it.

Mom's at her desk. Dad's at the stove.
Are you hungry, honey?

I imagine the taste of the familiar foods
soft-salty cheese and crunchy-grainy crackers
crisp and juicy end of winter pear.

I shake my head no.
My stomach squeals.

Are you sure? Mom stops her grading.
Yes, I promise. I'm sure. I had a lot for lunch.
Mom turns back to her pile of papers.
The lie screams inside.

Different

Amaya says she feels completely different
because she's lost seven pounds.

She can't tell me how, exactly,
just different, and I wonder because

I feel different, too—
dizzy, hungry, tired, nothing on my mind but food.

Dani points as I pull on my gym shorts—
You look exactly the same!

I hold up my gym shirt
like a shield against her eyes,

as self-conscious as ever.

Maybe more.

Costume

Mom and I head out after dinner
searching for fabric she'll sew
into a swaying skirt for my solo.

Periwinkle and pale green shimmery fabric,
on sale and perfectly
drapey and swishy.

Perfect. Mom will make it sway and swirl
in the breeze of me
when I dance in May.

Pincushion

Mom pins here and there
wrapping, draping,

adjusting, estimating
what to do to get exactly what I want

but I look up into the mirror
pinned-up shimmer

makes me look
like a blue and green bubble.

This is awful—I hate it!
Take it off! I can't wear it!

Mom sighs and rewraps it, then points to the mirror.
That's how it will look when it's finished, she says.

I stare with a pout
at the mirror and her
and the stupid costume.

Her face says,
You can say you're sorry anytime now.
But I don't.

Forever

Makela says she's on a new diet with her mom
It's a non-diet diet, and it's really going to work.

They buy all kinds of food from the diet.
They've promised themselves new outfits at the end.

She says she's lucky her mom understands.
But still. Why don't they buy new outfits now?

They could use the money they're spending
on all the "non-diet" diet food.

Dani says she cheated all week, but now she's "good".
She lost three pounds but gained back five.

My brain goes crazy hearing this.
That was my diet too—I was afraid to say it—

feeling lighter at first, then so hungry
I couldn't help buying snacks,

stuffing them down
without tasting.

Even though we have no scale
I knew I was bigger by my jeans' zipper.

Amaya says she'll have to stay in control all the time.
She'll lose weight and gain it back, like her mom.

But she'll lose it again, no prob.
That's what happens all the time, she says.
That's the way it is.

All the time seems awfully long.
All the time means forever.

Thief

Jules, away again.
Door closed to guard her life from me.

I walk in anyway. There's her bowl of rose petals
from an old bouquet given as she stood in a spotlight.

I lift one and sniff, want to keep it for a dried-out souvenir
but drop it in the bowl. The sound is a whisper.

Wall plastered with articles, photographs
from her first play to last.

I press my palm against a photo—
Jules taking a bow at the end of a show,

the spotlight a cone-shape around her,
my fingers outline the light on paper

as if I might steal it
and make it mine.

Frizz

My frizz muddles the glittery stars
I tuck in my hair. I miss Beck.

Maybe I'll ask Mom to straighten my hair.
Don't even think about it, she'll say. *Beautiful the way it is.*

I head downstairs and pass Mom at her desk.
I scare her with *You know, you don't really want me to grow up.*

She stares with a what-did-I-do-now look
but I know she can read my mind.

On and On, and On

Tonight at the Shabbat table
Jules goes on and on. And on—
about this person's costume and that person's makeup
in *A Midsummer Night's Dream*
and a scene she does
where there's a kiss
and she's so-o-o-o-o-o embarrassed
because her boyfriend's there watching
and
blah
blah
blah.

I scrape my knife and fork
through the fish, so soft
it doesn't need the noise.

I stare at my plate.
Try to shut my ears
from the inside.

Then I clatter
the fork and knife,
scrape my chair away from the table
May I please be excused?
I don't recognize my loud voice

but I'm gone without an answer,
slamming the basement door
against all the noise
of my un-listening family.

Tug of War

Jules' door is open this morning.
I walk in before I chicken out.
Can I borrow a scarf? comes out of my mouth.
Face in her phone, Jules points toward the closet.

I enter the dim light of her forest of scarves,
pull out a grey and teal—silky, soft, delicate,
swishing back and forth on my arms,
raising goose bumps. *Can you help me?*

She sighs and lifts her face to me.
I'm as still as a member of a waiting corps de ballet
while she hums and flips, pulls, circles
my neck and arranges the scarf.

There, she says. *That's pretty.*
She smiles. My heart warms up.
She's my Jules again.
I almost hug her.

Just don't ruin it, she says and turns away.
My heart crashes.
I tug the scarf off, throw it at the floor.
You're such a jerk, Jules!

She sighs and says, *Oh, Reeni, don't be such a baby*
in her sweet, soft voice.

She shakes her big wavy hair,
swinging it like a shampoo ad

so I grab it
and pull, pull, PULL!

Get out, you baby! Jules screams at me.
And leave me alone!

Another Solo in My Future

Next to Beck in Hebrew school.
She stares at the board,

a chart with sounds.
They go with the words

we learn from the Torah.
The cantor sings through

the sounds for the vowels,
shapes and dots marked on the page

we've learned for our b'nei mitzvah.
How will I do it? How can it be

that there's another solo
in store for me?

Jason Says

Reeni, you have a beautiful voice.

What a jerk.

At Night

Mom eyes my plate at dinner
as I swirl the cheese lasagna into designs.

I fill my plate
with a huge second helping
as if to say, *See? I'm eating!*

and gobble it down
so she'll leave me alone.

Ugh

I'm so full I roll on the floor
in my room back and forth,

scrunch up in a ball
hold my stomach,

press it in, push at the pain.
Aaaaaaah. Ooooooooh. Nnnnnnnnn.

Two huge helpings of sloppy, cheesy, saucy lasagna.
I never knew I could eat that much.

I imagine Makela, Dani, and Amaya
eyes wide at my confession about stuffing lasagna

into myself, saying what they say: *I'm so disgusting.*
Promising myself never to do it again.

Not Listening

Mom sits me down to talk
Reeni, you're not listening to me.

(I don't say: *Mom, you didn't listen to me.*)

*You've been picking at meals
then stuffing yourself.*

(I don't say: *I told you I had to fix myself.*)

I shrug, can't look Mom in the eyes
but say, *Dancers don't look like me.*

Mom's face gets sad.
As long as you keep dancing, they do, she says.

Brain Noise

At Ms. Allie's I'm full of whirling
thoughts of how to stop eating
too much when I'm hungry

a stranger inside me
who's taken control,
just as noisy as my fear used to be

I can't pay attention anymore,
the mess in my brain pounding
like music I'd never dance to.

Where's Jules?

Shabbat is here, but Jules is not.
Not here to share our blessing,

not here for Shabbat dinner?
Mom and Dad share a look

before they surround me
settle warm hands on my head

bless me
alone.

Babysitting

*Are you a ballerina? Mama says you are and
I want to be a ballerina too, so are you?
Are you?* She finally breathes.

Not yet, I say. *I'm learning to be one.*
I like how that sounds.
Should we read a book?

No. Can you practice ballet with me?
Her dark, deep eyes stare into mine,
making me important.

I grab a small chair from the kitchen
and turn it into Serena's barre.
I stand next to her, hand on the counter

and model first position, feet, legs, arms
then turn to her, mold her arms
with Ms. Allie's soft touch

round but not a circle,
soft but strong,
bent elbows, but not sharp

and feet turned out—
I nudge her curled-up toes—
Heels together, there you go.

She flashes a smile:
Am I a ballerina now?
Almost, I say.

Another Hungry Night

Eyes closed
stomach growling

out of bed
in a quiet minute

Jules' light shining
into the hall

down the stairs two at a time
softly, toe-touch, heel-light into the kitchen.

Fridge hums. Door opens: cheese invites me—
Eat! Eat! Eat!

One corner. Two.
Three.

Then a huge chunk.

Like a Mouse

Scurrying upstairs
like a mouse in a picture book
nibbling cheese
but not cute.

What are you doing?
Jules stands in a long line of light from her door.

Trapped!

I push her away,
fast-close my door
against her lit face

my mouth full of cheese
and me, hating myself
and not cute.

Not cute at all.

Jules Butts In

Know-it-all Jules walks in
uninvited.

Reeni, I'm worried.
Please tell me what's up.

Like a person who doesn't love her,
I say, *None of your business.*

She sits on my bed,
puts her hand on my shoulder.

Come on, Reeni—
you can talk to me.

But I roll away, her touch a reminder
that she'll be gone, that she's been away.

I pull blankets over my head
and squeeze tears back

until she sighs
and leaves.

What They See

I'm up in front of class again
with Dhara, Lacey, Rosana, and Sasha
who's staring at my butt, I'm sure.

She must be wondering
how it's gotten bigger,
how I dare to dance with it

but at least they can't see
what a jerk I am dieting to lose weight
and gaining it instead.

Too Tight!

Upstairs in my room I pull on
my now-beautiful blue and green costume

over my head and chest—
too tight!

I fill up with some kind
of boiling liquid

and pull at my costume
almost rip it

as I escape from it, throw it, stomp it
down on the floor.

Tantrum

Mom!
MOM!!!

Face red.
Soaked with tears.

Stomping.
Mom's there in a minute.

She's quiet. Holds me.
Don't worry, I'll fix it.

Jules stands in the hallway
watching it all, shaking her head.

Go away! I shout.
I hate you!

Still holding me in a tight grip
Mom closes the door.

Mom's Arms

She hugs me, holds me
Reeni, you're beautiful.

I don't believe her,
but I don't want to tell her,

don't want to be anywhere
but inside her arms.

Trying to Diet Again

Test tomorrow,
can't study this way,

legs jiggling, nails bitten,
no history staying in my brain,

too crowded
with hunger.

Up and Down Again

In dance class my eyes run up and down

up
and
down,
down
and
up
Sasha's
long lean landscape

wishing
it was mine,

still half-believing
the courage I need
is called
"thin."

Hiding

It's late at night
and Jules isn't home yet.

Not home yet.
Mom and Dad share a look

before they say goodnight
and think I'm in bed.

Sad and Glad

I'm upstairs when Jules comes home.
I hear Dad stop her—*Hold on, Jules.*

We need to talk.
I lean over the railing.
You're never around.
You need to drop something.
We got a call from school
and your grades are down.

I hear whining,
stomping,
crying.

Dad says, *Your agreement for the scholarship*
is that you keep grades up.
Your final semester still counts.
And—your sister still needs you, too.

Sobbing.

It feels bad
to be secretly
glad.

Awake

I hear Jules crying
in her room, tiny private sobs
that seep through the wall
between us

and I remember the times
she made me feel better
and press my cheek
against the wall

like a long-distance
hug.

Tickets!

Mom's home from Sunday shopping
smiling, handing me an envelope.

Swan Lake—just you and me, downtown. Today!
I'm buzzing inside. Jumping outside.

Swan Lake? Are you kidding?
The real ballet? How could we afford it?

I grab a chair
so I won't fly away!

Auditorium

It's a palace, crystal chandeliers shooting rainbows,
golden trim all around us.

Me in a bright blue dress with covered buttons,
dress shoes and a blue pashmina.

Mom's got my hand and steers me through
skinny girls in pink tights and leotards under skirts.

Did they all come from a class, or are they saying,
Look, I'm a dancer.

If I told them I'm one too,
would they believe me?

Inside

Shimmery blue-greens, purples, dark shadows
surround us, tucked into our velvety seats.
It's dark now—then the spotlight.

The Sorcerer's behind the curtain
and a shadow princess becomes a swan.

Now he comes out with a real swan!
The huge wings open, and it tries to fly.
I grab the edges of my seat
as my stomach drops and the curtain rises.

Oh!

My heart leaps out to whirl onstage
with corps de ballet in purples, blues, greens, pinks,
skirts split and pointe shoes kicking out,

lost in the music along with them
as they twirl on pointe, run-run-leap,
then lean onto danseurs' strong arms for arabesque.

Then I notice bodices above the skirts—one, four, ten,
twenty:
flat and hard, straight across,

no breasts, tiny waists, strong arms,
shoulder to shoulder bone.

I can't breathe. My eyes zigzag
from one dancer to the other,

looking and looking for signs of roundness.
Anything. Anywhere. Nowhere. Now I'm shaking.

There's no one like me.
The screams in my head
are louder than music.

LOUD, HUGE VOICE

"You'll never fit in. No costume will fit you. No danseur can lift you. A body like yours has no place here at all."

Blur

My brain's numb,
face hot,
can't feel,
can't see.

Why did Mom bring me?
Did she want me to see

that no matter what I try
I will never be like them?

Nasty

Thanks, Mom.
Thanks a lot.

My body's a rock
as I stare out my window
all the way home.

Some Other Girl

In the basement at night,
fierce fighter, not dancer

with a noisy brain
practicing the solo

someone else
should perform.

Traitors

Letting sweat drip,
climbing stairs
to shower before bed,

whispers in Mom's and Dad's room—
I listen outside the door.

She throws out her lunch, Jules says.
I called Beck—she told me.
She sneaks downstairs when you're in bed...
Some crazy diet...

Her voice gets louder.
You think it's not possible,
just because you see her gaining weight
and not losing?
She's crying.
It's partly my fault.
I should have listened.

I jump into the shower before they come out,
turn the water hot enough to sting me numb.

Too Heavy

They're downstairs when I get out of the shower.
I jump into bed, turn out the light, pretend I'm asleep.

When the door opens, I turn away
weighed down with my secrets

too heavy for a girl.

Out of School

Mom shows up at school and takes me out.
We're going to the doctor.

I pull away. *I don't want to go! I have my class!*

You're throwing out lunches,
picking at dinners, stuffing yourself.
I saw it, but I couldn't believe it.

I stomp all the way down the hall.
I'll stop! I promise! As soon as I lose what I gained!

We're going. That's all.
You have no choice.

Angry

I slam down my books
head out to the car

pull the door open
flounce into my seat

tug my seatbelt into place
twist toward the window

away from Mom.

What the Doctor Says

She's not interested in my size or shape.
She's interested in my health.
She wants me to relax about food.
That's how you've always eaten—why change now?

I don't say:
Has she seen the magazines?
Does she use the internet?

Everything that's happening to your body
is perfectly normal. I know this for sure.

I don't say:
You don't get it, either.
Everything happening to my body
feels perfectly crazy.

Trapped

The diet works, then doesn't.
My jeans get a tiny bit loose,
then refuse to zip

and I'm just as afraid to solo
as I ever was.

Liar

I tell Mom I'll stop doing what I've been doing.

I don't tell her my plan is to do it better.

Just until my solo.

Fight

Loud voices downstairs, Mom and Dad.
You should have waited to talk to me first, Mira.

David, she needed help with this, so I took her to the doctor.
I lean to listen, tiptoe across my room to the stairs.

You should have talked to me first. We should have decided together.
Their voices soften. I hang over the railing—

Mom—*Worried...*
Dad—*Smart...she'll stop.*

Mom—*have to...pay attention...*
What does that mean?

Dad—*depends what kind of attention...More harm than good.*
Not right. We make decisions together.

Then it's quiet. I worry.

Let's stop now, Dad says. *Mira, let's stop.*
You're right. You're right. I'm sorry.

I hear them moving across the floor, into the hall.
Are they hugging?

I hope they're hugging.
I want them to be hugging.

Why are you so angry at her? Dad's voice is soft,
Mom bangs her hand down.

I thought she was safe. I thought we were different.
I'm angry at myself, not Reeni. I couldn't see what was happening.

She's crying now. *I couldn't protect her.*
Is it ballet? Should she stop?

Don't, Dad says, *don't say that.*
It's not just ballet. You know it can happen to anyone.

Not Hungry

I hate myself.

When they're all asleep I sneak downstairs, pull out leftovers, sit and wait and then as if some green light signals, Go! I stuff myself with meat and potatoes and pasta and sauce and chocolate and pudding and onions and carrots and I eat with my fingers with sauce running down scooping and shoving things into my mouth as if I'm a cave or an empty cavern,
a hole with no bottom.

Now I'm sick.

Now I hate myself even more.

Never

Silent, stomping, slamming upstairs.
I turn the lock,
whisper-scream at the mirror, *I hate you! I hate you!*

I rip my clothes off,
fingers poke and pinch,
push at bulges
pound,
pound,
punch.

Hate myself. Hurt myself,
digging my nails in until I leave marks.

Grab my robe, collapse in a corner,
silent sobbing,
sobbing.
It will never end.

The ballerinas on my wall gaze down and laugh.
You'll never be like us.
Never.
Never.
Never.

Rolling Rock

There's a rock behind my eyes
rolling downhill
into my throat
and
down
down
into
my
stomach

already full
and then it grows   grows   grows
expanding the edges of me
until I'm a huge balloon
and explode

and all my pieces
blow away.

Pieces

I'm on the floor in the middle of the night,
hurting, trying to sob away the hurt, wide awake.

Mom's voice presses in from the other side of the door,
soft, warm. I roll away to let her in

and she drops to the floor and crumples me gently
into her hugging arms.

I cuddle close. *I can't dance anymore.*
I cough out the words.

Mom wipes my face, my hair. She's crying now.
She's mad, but not at me.

She holds my face between her hands
and I can't escape her eyes.

I won't let you do this to yourself.
She holds me tighter and I scrunch into her lap

that's always been mine, sob till I sleep,
Mom's hand soft on my head.

But even that gentle hand can't sew
all the ripped pieces of me together.

Stupid Diet

It would take a person
without a brain

not to see I'm eating more
than I ever ate before.

List Examples of the Following Parts of Speech and Writing

Adjectives

Stuffed.
Heavy.
Ugly.
Bad.

Similes

Stuffed as Dad's peppers that burst in the oven.
Heavy as the stack of books I carry from the library.
Ugly as...
Ugly as it's possible to be.

Bad as
I've ever been.

Punctuation Marks

Stupid!
Why did you do this?

Just stop it!

Math in Everyday Life

Mr. Salazar's talking
about least common multiples
and how math is useful
in everyday life.

How true: my time has gone
to adding up calories for food I sneak,
subtracting what I haven't eaten
from what I might eat,

multiplying the number of lies
I've told Mom and Dad,
dividing days left
into will I or won't I dance?

Again

Some older boy whispers to Jason
who stands by my locker,
nudging him, nodding,
pointing at me.

My legs want to take me
a different direction.
Noise rings in my ears
and the hall seems to twirl.

I try to ignore him,
lean into my locker,
open it, reach inside
finding my book.

Hey, Reeni, says Jason.
The boy stares at my chest,
tells Jason to look at my sparkly new blouse.

Jason looks at the ceiling,
Jason looks down the hall.
But Jason doesn't say, *Stop it.*
Jason doesn't say anything at all.

Worst Day of My Life

Ms. Allie's elegant arm invites me to begin
rehearsing my solo, everyone watching.

She starts the music and I can't run away—
my head's full of awful words: chubby, awkward, ugly.

I try to fight the words: *I'm beautiful the way I am!*
and force pointed toes, perfect arms.

Music prickles, doesn't flow.
I pull myself tight, find a spot for turns

but I'm dizzy, off-balance, twisting, tipping.
stumbling, hopping—

I trip
tip

crash
on my ankle.

Can't move.

Can't disappear.

Out the Window

The doctor wraps my ankle,
unbroken but a grade one sprain.

One week off the foot for sure.
Rest, ice, bandage.
No dancing.
No dancing?

Rolling clouds, pouring rain
turns into a gale, too dark for a rainbow.

Dad says, *Spring in Chicago.*
Scary how relieved I feel.

I Can Do It

I insist that I can babysit
with my wrapped foot
and spend half an hour
washing chocolate out of Serena's hair
because she won't stop talking.
Can you still do your solo?
What will happen if you can't?
Will you still be Ballerina Reeni if you don't?
I have to go potty. Do you have to go potty?
Do you want to try?

I yell, *Stop it!*
and her face wilts,
her little chin quivers.

Serena, I'm sorry, I'm really sorry.
I kneel to her height. She grins at my apology:
I'm okay. I really am.
But are you okay?

I nod and wipe my eyes, wet from scaring her,
yelling at a little kid's questions
I'm afraid to answer.

I Can't Do It

Clumping over to Ms. Allie's.
Have to get there before class.

Little kids like multicolored bubbles pop out the door.
Does one of them dream of the spotlight?

Kick shoes off. Search for Ms. Allie.
She finds me first. She takes my hand. I look away.

I'm too scared to do it.
I'm quitting I'm sorry I don't want to dance.

I pull my hand but she holds on tight
the way I used to grab the barre before I could balance.

How do you know you can't do the solo?
How do you know if you've never tried?

I can't. I can't.
I pull away my hand.

I can't.

What Grownups Say

Ms. Allie's soft words walk home with me.
Grown-ups say pretty things in quiet voices.

You're beautiful the way you are.
How do you know if you've never tried?

The words are kind.
The words sound right

but they don't solve my problem.
What happened to my Still, Small Voice?

Not Scared Anymore

Sitting on the floor downstairs.
No dancing.
No worries.
No knots in my stomach.
No Loud, Huge Voice.

Blank brain.

Just wishing
the Still, Small Voice

could make me
not care.

Memory—Like That

I remember a day long ago in a field
between mountains, we stopped when our ears popped.
I jumped from the car and ran toward a forest
where snow on the trees seemed so odd in the summer.

Faster and faster, speeding across,
lungs filling, pushing, I thought I would fly.

Dancing was like that.
The space between mountains
where flying was a possible dream.

Fly, fly! I remember the sound
like a whisper in my ears only.

When You're Old

Did you dance your solo yet?
Serena's in footed pajamas

bouncing
bouncing
bouncing.

I shake my head.
I can't tell her I quit.

It's okay. I'll go and see you.
I'll be good luck. Daddy says so.

I ask her: what if I decide not to do it?
You'll be old and sad, Daddy says.

But don't worry because then
I will take care of you!

Passover Seder

Every year we retell the story
of the ancient Israelites escaping slavery

and Dad and Mom add stories of today,
slavery now, people trapped, hurt, killed:

Dad says, *We must all help to heal the world.*
By the time we eat it's feeling crazy

that I've spent this year thinking about food,
as if "thin" would be a magic trick

to make me someone
I think I want to be

or give me the courage
that's out of reach for me.

By Now I Think I Know

Diets are forever because:

You diet and get too hungry.
You eat too much because you're too hungry.
You diet again because you ate too much,
because you're too hungry.

The diet was like my wild spinning bourrée turns,
not spotting where I was going,
off-balance but unable to stop till I fell.

Maybe the Still, Small Voice
is here, deep inside, with me always
speaking the words I'm hearing now:

My rounder thighs didn't steal the way I dance.
My curvy hips won't ruin my turns.
My growing breasts won't hold me down.

I don't have too much body.
I have too little courage.
Which I guess I always knew.

Mess and Un-Mess

In the kitchen—Mom, Dad, me.
I'm pulling at the elastic of my ballet slipper.

I pull until stitches pop.
I'm sorry I lied to you.

The elastic pops away from my slipper.
I messed everything up.

They hug me hard.
Growing up is messy.

I love that I don't have to say more.
I love that I have more to say.

Apologies

Beck sees me at my locker
and bumps through the crowd when I signal her.

She's two feet away. I find words I need.
I'm not being stupid anymore.

She nods. *I'm sorry I had to tell Jules.*
But I was scared you'd hurt yourself.

The space between us feels like a mile.
Will someone erase it?

I take a step forward.
I wish you hadn't left me alone
even though you were mad.

She steps toward me. *I'm sorry,* she says
and the rest of our distance disappears.

No More

Dani raises her eyebrows
when she sees my sandwich.
I'm not dieting anymore, I say.

She rolls her eyes.
Your choice. She sniffs.

I say out loud:
There's nothing wrong with me.

Dani laughs.
Good luck with that!
She turns away.

I'm hungry. I eat.
It feels just right.

Wishes

Mom wishes

she could tell me I would never
feel pressure to be anyone
except myself.

She wishes

magazines and commercials and movies
would show all kinds of bodies
all colors, sizes, shapes, abilities.

She wishes

I'd stop wishing I was like Jules,
outgoing and eager to perform.

She wishes

she didn't have to wish these things
at all.

I hope
that Mom
can see

I wish to make my own wishes
come true.

For Myself

After days of no dancing I head downstairs.
Have I been hiding from myself,
starving for music?

I hum *Swan Lake* and sway and rock
until my arms float up
and my legs must move.

I pose, I run
and leap as high as ever,
arms wide, then soft and flowing

as I land, each step automatic,
then catch my breath
and whirl again.

Turning toward the music,
music like the Still, Small Voice
carries me through the air
dancing and believing.

From the Beginning

It was there from my birth
is what my dad says,

there in my crib
when babies don't care
how big or small or round they are,

when they don't care if they're shy
or bold,

there from my birth,
loving to move, moving to music,

there from my birth
and here again, now.

Now Jules

Upstairs again, Jules stops me.
Reeni, can I talk to you?
She reaches to hug me but I hold back.

I'm sorry, Jules says.
I didn't try hard enough to help you.

She hugs me like nothing kept us apart,
and this time I hug back. Something opens inside.

What am I going to do without you next year?
There, I said it. And tears I was trying never to cry

rush out with relief that starts me shivering
in the spring breeze.

Jules holds on tight,
and I know that Michigan won't be too far away.

Before Candlelighting

Wanting to dance, wanting to hide.
Which one is stronger?

Mom lights the candles,
and the flames glow.

Inside, I feel their reflection,
hear the Still, Small Voice:
Listen.

Jules and I bow our heads.
Mom and Dad recite the blessing:

May you be like Sarah, Rebecca, Rachel, and Leah.
May God bless you and guard you.
May God show you favor and be gracious to you.
May God show you kindness and grant you peace.

Me in My Room

Spring air curls through my bedroom window,
circles around me,
turns me to the scent of neighbors' early gardens.

My body is blossoming, maybe I'm blossoming too,
becoming someone
I don't know yet, but still me.

I pull out my ballet slippers
to mend the ripped elastic.

Is That Me Talking?

In school today Jason's alone.
He sees me see him, starts across the hall.

I feel like running but stand strong,
nudging my eyes to look into his.

I have the exact words I need:
Leave me alone, Jason.

He turns bright red, stares at the floor,
mumbles, *I'm sorry.*

I shake my head. He raises his.
I'm really sorry. I won't do it again.

I have nothing to say to that

right now.

Small Step

I slip my costume off its hanger,

wriggle into it, pose, hum *Swan Lake*.
Soft against my skin,
silky in my hands.

I point and pose, then step, step, step,
arms in familiar shapes, flowing.

The Still, Small Voice says,
Dance, Reeni—dance.

Still Awake

I run downstairs to dance again,
moving the way I was born to move,
love to move—point, plié, pirouette,

stretch into arabesque.
My solo unfolds like Odette's swan wings,
but not Odette.

Now it's me, Reeni, dancing,
starting over then over again
until aching and dripping,

dropping one last curtsy.

The Loud, Huge Voice!

"Last night the dance world saw the debut of young
prodigy Reeni Rosenbloom and it's hard to believe
what happened to this amazing dancer! In spite
of all her preparations and the encouragement
she has gotten from family and friends, she leaped
onto the stage and as she looked out
into the audience, froze! She had to be removed
from the stage by her red-faced, elderly teacher.
How embarrassing for all concerned!"

The Still, Small Voice

Still, Small Voice whispers,
It's not true.

And I believe it.

Maybe

One deep breath.

My leg points, arms float.
I pose.
I dance.

I pretend
there's an audience
and my body goes cold.

But I keep on,
dance it away.

Is it a hint,
a touch as soft
as a worn pink ballet shoe

pointing my way ahead?

Return

I lean on the barre to wait for Ms. Allie,
windows open to the spring breeze,
music blaring from a passing car.

I'm still—watching, listening.

Paint's peeling off window sills,
a dust bunny hiding where floor and wall meet,
spaces between the wood slats I've danced on
for seven years.

I hear Ms. Allie's soft footsteps,
I push away from the barre,
heart wild, stomach twirling.

I breathe and hear my Still, Small Voice:
Turn, Reeni, turn—
Turn now, and ask.

I do.
And Ms. Allie says, *Yes.*

Before

No music, settled into quiet stretching,
then backbend without hands,
Ms. Allie and me,

she looks into my eyes,
hands circling my back, not holding, but tapping—
Right here, I'm right here.

The
lowest
point
of
my
spine

is the center. I backward-bend
drawing a careful circle
tracing my head
to the floor

all moving muscle, one thought, one word.
Safe.
I am safe, right here with her,
Ms. Allie protecting but letting me guide.

She's here if I need her
but I'm steady and strong

in the circle
of her untouching arms.

Just Step Out

Who I am tonight,
is a changed Reeni, but the same,

growing myself
into who I might become

if I can only step out
into the spotlight.

One Second Before

Dark, can't see the stage floor,
reach for Ms. Allie,
right there.

Her hands on my hips,
she turns me and whispers,
Straight ahead ten steps, pose and lift your face to the audience.

My slippers touch with a gentle sound
only I hear—one step, two, three, four, five.
I fill my lungs—six, seven, eight—and breathe out.

I smooth my skirt. Do they hear me now?
Nine steps, ten. Turn and pose,
arms up and out, soft, strong, tilt my head.

The curtain rises.
I lift my face to the audience,
eyes scanning the front row.

There's Mom and Dad.
And Jules.
And Beck.
And Jason, sitting next to Beck.
And little Serena,
dressed in a tutu.

Star

Point-press, point-press, point-press.
The harp notes begin, the spotlight brightens.

My legs are strong and graceful,
my arms are wings,
my bourrée turns are tiny and tight.

The music fills me like air and blood
and I dance for myself, with everyone watching.
Courage was right here, waiting for me.

Maybe only tonight, maybe always,
the courage I needed is deep inside
somewhere I couldn't reach before,

unlocked by listening,
sending a message controlled but loose,
strong but flowing—

Dance!

Music flows through me—it always will—
I glow in the lights,
shine like one little star in the universe

from this small stage
all the way
to the edges of the sky.

Acknowledgments

During the writing of *Reeni's Turn,* more friends and colleagues than I can mention offered information, support, and encouragement, invaluable experiences for a writer.

Special thanks to Jaynie Royal, publisher and editor-in-chief of Regal House Publishing, and editor Elizabeth Lowenstein. Jaynie's perceptiveness, kindness, efficiency, professionalism, and communicativeness made the journey from manuscript to book a pleasure.

Heartfelt thanks to Emma Dryden for the straightforward, challenging professional critique of an early draft that pushed me to become a better writer and more honest poet.

Readers and writers who played critical roles in this story's development are Ami Polonsky, Lisa Jenn Bigelow, Lisa Sukenic, Claudia Mills, Ellen Reagan, Brenda Ferber, Jenny Meyerhoff, Carolyn Crimi, Esther Hershenhorn, Irma Crump, Rebecca Coven, and Judith Matz. For wonderful specifics, I thank Judy Wolkin, Fayge Miriam Crandus, and Karin Klein.

Irene Sufrin, friend and skilled, creative educator, opened a life-changing door to me at the Skokie Solomon Schechter Day School Learning Center and cheered my journey through joy and disappointment with unfailing encouragement.

Carol Munter opened another life-changing door that guided me to a life uncluttered by discomfort and despair about body size and food. My gratitude for this is unending.

Ellen Holtzblatt, visual artist, colleague, and friend: thanks for our wonderful conversations about the challenges and joys of creative work, and so much more.

To my small family of writer-supportive siblings, cousins, nieces and nephews: I thank you and love you.

To my husband Bob and son Adam: I love you dearly—wherever I turn, you are my "spots."